S0-BRI-500

LIGHTHOUSE

A Story of Remembrance

For Sarah Gillis, Antigonish, Nova Scotia.
— R.M.

For my husband, Chris, with love always, and with thanks for his support.
Thanks also to my models, Juliana and Pat.
— J.W.

The illustrations for this book were painted in oils on canvas.

This book was designed in QuarkXPress, with type set in 15 point Goudy Old Style.

National Library of Canada Cataloguing in Publication

Munsch, Robert N., 1945-
Lighthouse : a story of remembrance / Robert Munsch ;
illustrated by Janet Wilson.

ISBN 0-439-97458-5

I. Wilson, Janet, 1952- II. Title.

PS8576.U575 L53 2003   jC813'.54   C2003-900610-7
                             PZ7

Text copyright © 2003 by Bob Munsch Enterprises Ltd.
Illustrations copyright © 2003 by Janet Wilson.
Title page drawing copyright © 2003 by Sarah Gillis.
All rights reserved.

No part of this publication may be reproduced or stored in a retrieval system, or transmitted in any form or by any means,
electronic, mechanical, recording, or otherwise, without written permission of the publisher,
North Winds Press, a division of Scholastic Canada Ltd., 175 Hillmount Road, Markham, Ontario L6C 1Z7, Canada.
In the case of photocopying or other reprographic copying, a licence must be obtained from
Access Copyright (Canadian Copyright Licensing Agency), 1 Yonge Street, Suite 1900,
Toronto, Ontario M5E 1E5 (1-800-893-5777)

6 5 4 3 2 1   Printed in Canada   03 04 05 06

Robert Munsch

LIGHTHOUSE

A *Story of Remembrance*

Illustrated by
Janet Wilson

North Winds Press
A Division of Scholastic Canada Ltd.

*I*n the middle of the night, Sarah woke up, put a
flower in her hair, and went into her mother and
father's bedroom. She sat on her father's side of the
bed for a long time. Finally he woke up and said,
"Sarah, what's going on? It's the middle of the night."

"Well," said Sarah, "you always told me how
Grandpa used to take you out to the lighthouse in
the middle of the night, and this is the middle
of the night, and tonight is the night to take me."

Her father lay still for a long time, and then he said,
"Yes, I think this is the night."

So they got dressed very quietly, went out to the
car, and drove off.

There was nobody else around.
No cars were out, and the
streetlights made the sea
fog glow.

"When Grandpa took me to
the lighthouse there were no
streetlights, and there were no
doughnut shops open in the
middle of the night," said
Sarah's father.

"But he would have stopped
if there had been doughnut
shops," said Sarah.

"Right," said her father.

So they stopped at a doughnut shop and bought a bag of maple icing doughnuts and some coffee. They were the only customers there.

"When I was little, Grandpa used to give me coffee, and it always tasted terrible," said Sarah's dad.

So they both drank some coffee for Grandpa. Dad's coffee tasted good, and Sarah's coffee tasted terrible.

Then they drove out of town
till they came to the road that
led to the lighthouse.

"Grandpa always said we should walk up the road to the lighthouse," said Sarah's father.

"Right," said Sarah.

So they parked the car and walked up through the fog to the lighthouse.

Then they sat on the top of the cliff above the beach and listened to the waves crash on the rocks. Sarah ate the doughnuts, and her father drank more coffee.

"All the times Grandpa took me with him," said Sarah's father, "we never once went up to the top of the lighthouse. The door was always locked. We tried to open it, but it was always locked."

"I'm going to try the door," said Sarah.

So she walked over and tried the knob, and the door opened. Sarah and her dad stood looking at the doorway.

"What now?" said Sarah.

"Grandpa would have gone up," said Sarah's father.

"So let's go up," said Sarah.

They walked up the winding staircase,

round and round and round and round,

until finally they stood in front of the light.

"I can see forever," said Sarah. "Can Grandpa see me?"

"I don't know," said her father.

"Can Grandpa hear me?" said Sarah. And she yelled really loud, "GRANDPA!"

They waited a long time.

"He's not going to answer," said her father.

They stood for a long time
and listened to the foghorn
and looked at the mist and
the ocean. Then Sarah took
the flower from her hair, the
flower she had saved from
her grandfather's funeral,
and threw it way out over
the ocean.

"When I grow up, I'm going to have a kid, and someday we will come here in the very middle of the night," said Sarah.

"Right," said her father.

And then, covered with dew from the fog
and smelling like seaweed, they went
home to bed.